The Journey Begins

by L.R. Mike "Mickey" Becker

This is one book you won't forget

Published by Luverne R. Becker, Minneapolis, MN

Printed in the United States of America
First Printing

ISBN 0-9676176-0-X

Dedication

I can only inadequately thank Richard "Pinky" McNamara and his wife, Sharon. If it wasn't for them, you wouldn't be reading this now. Also a heartfelt thank you to Bill Kauffmann.

This book is dedicated to my precious wife and family and to all my loved ones and friends.

Cathy;
I hope that you find the journey worth while my old friend.
Much love,
Mickey

Introduction

The poems you are about to read reflect the story of my life and some of the events that have taken place during it, or they capture a mood or a human emotion. Sit back, relax, listen and feel. The journey begins.

Contents

Part II: A Love Affair

Part III: Thorns and Roses

Part IV: Laughter and Tears

Part V: Nearing the Journey's End

Part I

From the Great Depression to Vietnam

The Great Depression

Central High Remembrances

I was the poorest dressed kid
Who ever attended Central High,
And I could get affidavits to attest
That fact is not a lie.
At the time I didn't know it,
But I could have pulled quite a plum,
For I could have sold my patched-up pants
To any clown, for quite a tidy sum.

I ate oatmeal for Thanksgiving dinner,
And for some suppers I just breathed the air,
But I didn't know I was underprivileged,
For poverty was everywhere.

I never attended a prom,
Or for that matter any dance;
My heart never felt the glow
Of a high school romance.
I never saw the look of love,
Nor felt the press of a hand
That implied the unspoken words
I care, I understand.

And as for the highlight of my social life,
I owe it all to my friend Jim.
And because of his kindness to me
I will always be indebted to him,
For he invited me to come along
Over to his girlfriend's house,
And I didn't even have to be
As quiet
As a
Mouse.

Jim Dickinson was the name of my friend. One day he put on the pair of pants that I wore to school and I ended up on the floor roaring with laughter. They had patches, on patches, on patches, etc. No clown ever had a better uniform or a better friend.

On the more positive side:

Our Gang

There was our gang,
Butsy, Chuck, Jim, Reed and Riley,
Just to name a few:
I must admit that we were a motley-looking crew.

We played football, baseball and softball,
And although we didn't look like much,
It didn't take our opponents long to discover
That we weren't a soft touch.

We had camaraderie,
We lived, we laughed, we cried
And we cared about each other
With a love that stemmed from deep inside.

Today thoughts about old friends
Help chase away the blues
When they walk across your mind
Wearing a pair of old tennis shoes.

Then came the war.

War through the eyes of a mother.

Ten Little Fingers

My beloved husband never saw the son I bore,
For he was killed during the final days of the Great War.

I had a son one cold December day that was bleak,
And soon I felt the touch of his ten little fingers upon my cheek.
Time passed so fast, how could it be?
Before I knew it my son was three.

Ten little fingers that grew and grew,
He was a man at last, I knew, I knew,
Gentle, tender, loving and kind,
This is what he became, this son of mine.

On graduation day I stood in the crowd,
Being his mother I couldn't help but feel proud,
And now this man who not so long ago had played hide-and-go-seek,
Once again placed his ten fingers upon my cheek.

But soon the bugles blew and the world went wild,
And another mother's son who no longer was a child
Placed his ten fingers upon his gun,
And took careful aim at my beloved son.

Yes, death, as it must to all men, came,
He was so young, yet just the same,
His voice was silenced, he will never speak,
Nor will I ever feel the touch of his ten fingers upon my check.

Now every Veterans Day after all has been said and done,
I can't held but think of the old cliché, "Like father, like son."

War through the eyes of a wife.

The Letter

My beloved husband,
I received your letter today,
And you made it seem just as though
You were a step away.

Yes, the war news does sound good,
It will be over soon, they say.
How David and Helen and I
Have been praying for that day.

David is hunting for his baseball,
Believe me, he is one of a kind,
Helen is writing you a little note
That I will enclose with mine.

All of the wonderful things your letter said,
I have placed them in the heart of me,
For as you know, long ago,
You became a part of me.

"Oh, excuse me, darling, the doorbell is ringing,
But I don't care, for my heart is singing."
And as she went to answer the door,
Thoughts of him accompanied her across the floor.

A messenger was waiting for her
With an envelope in his hand.
And as you know, some telegrams can warm you,
But this one began, "We regret to inform you."

When I was in grade school, we bought lead soldiers at the dime store. Years later, when I went overseas and I saw the massive cemeteries of the First World War dead, those two distant events intertwined and resulted in this.

Toy Soldiers

I dreamt I walked through Flanders Field
And like banners that became unfurled,
I heard the voices of the dead,
Begging me to say this to the world:

In the stores you can see toy soldiers
That little boys' hands will soon hold.
If I could take them all away,
I would recast them in a different mold.

I would make a few of them
Who stood erect and tall,
And several buglers who blew Taps
That echoed down the hall.

But I would cast many others
So their young eyes would see
The haggard face of war
Become a reality.

I would cast some without a leg,
And others who were blind,
And some of them without an arm,
This is what I had in mind.

And after I had used
Just a small portion of the lead,
I would cast toy soldiers,
Soldiers who were dead.

I specifically wrote the following poem with one general in mind but after I read a book about him I discovered that he was more to be pitied than censured.

[Note: In the military the word oblique is pronounced "o-blike"—it rhymes with "like."]

The Generals

When we were young we played a game of war
With toy soldiers that we bought at the dime store.
We built our fortresses out of sand
And as generals we barked out every command.
We used marbles for shot and shell,
And we fought until the enemy fell.
But one thing nice when we were through,
We could stand them up and start anew.

When we grew up a real war came,
And the generals commanded us to kill or maim,
And that we did until millions fell
And the earth became a living hell.
Retreat! Attack! Forward march! Left oblique!
My best friend was blown to bits,
And I never met a general that I liked.

I wrote the following poem after I saw the ravages of war.

Doves

Up with the doves,
Down with the warriors.
We need more peacemakers,
We have enough destroyers.

The rooster of death continued to crow loudly over the battlefield. Each morning he awoke with bloodshot eyes until the sweet sounding word peace finally became a reality. The war was over.

The Homecoming

After I came home from overseas,
I went to church and I fervently asked for His pardon
For during the war I saw why
He banished us from the Garden.

Some of Us

Some of us were like a whipped pup
Some of us were lifting too many a cup
Some of us were starting school
Some of us were playing the fool
Some of us were taking a bride
Some of us were hurting inside
Some of us had been through hell
Some of us went into a shell
Some of us laughed out loud
Some of us were alone in a crowd
Some of us became very bold
Some of us looked far too old
Some of us bought a brand-new Ford
Some of us talked about the good Lord
Some of us had even acquired a brand-new nickname
But one thing for sure, not one of us
Would ever be the same.

My Mother

My mother died when I was seven,
And they told me that she had gone to heaven.
They took her to the town where she was born
For her funeral one cold December morn.

I didn't know much about death, only angels in the sky,
I remember at her funeral I pinched myself so I would cry.
Maybe I was trying to block her death from my mind,
I don't think I ever meant to be that cold or unkind.

And even though her soul was saved
She was buried in a pauper's grave.
Years later my sister and her husband bought her a headstone
So that she would no longer lie there and be unknown.

Ah, but when my pa was playing baseball and traveling across the land,
She was constantly reaching out for his hand.
We stayed at Grandma's while he was gone,
And she would go to the Victrola and play just one song.

She played "Carolina Moon" deep into the night,
Until she finally turned off the light.
I recall how she would sit there, listen and sigh,
And years later, when I heard the lyrics, I knew the reason why.

And as for me, she loved me more than I can say,
For I had many a shirt torn off while playing pump-pump-pull-away;
And when I came home from school I never heard a harsh word,
The sound of love was all that I ever heard.

After the war I went to visit the grave
Of the woman who had given me life.
And as I dusted off the memories
That I had placed on a distant shelf,
With each one the tears overflowed,
And I didn't have to pinch myself.

Anna Emilie Ebert Becker, I love you.

The courtship of Mercedes Esther Larsen.

The Only One

My heart had a love song
That wanted to be sung,
But that seems so long ago
I forgot that I was still young.

My heart kept on waiting,
But when no love came its way
It just used that additional time
To store up more things to say.

But a heart does get lonely
When love keeps passing it by,
While it's eagerly waiting
To give love a try.

Then you came along
And made my heart glisten,
For you were the only one
Who took the time to listen.

The More I Know You

The more I know you
The more I'm aware
That this heart of mine
Is beginning to care.

The more I know you,
The more I can see
That this heart of mine
Doesn't want to be free.

The touch of your hand,
Your voice soft and low,
The way that I feel
When you have to go.

You make me happy,
My heart is aglow,
This love of mine
It's beginning to show.

Captured

You captured part of my heart
A little at a time,
Until I discovered
That it was no longer mine.

And we plighted our troth and we became one.

In the Eyes of the World

I was a dreamer when I was young,
I was the master of that art.
I placed myself in many a scene,
For I directed every part.
I was that knight in shining armor,
Or the hero of the game:
The plaudits of the crowd were mine,
And so were fortune and fame.
But when I set my dreams aside
What did I see,
When I stopped and looked into
The face of reality?

In the eyes of the world
I am nothing to see:
No banners have ever
Been unfurled for me.

In the eyes of the world
I would never be missed,
For in the eyes of the world
I don't even exist.

But in the eyes of my love
I am silver and gold,
I am the treasure
That she longs to hold.

In the eyes of the world
I'll never cause a stir,
But in the eyes of my love
I am the world to her.

But then my world fell apart.

I Just Can't Seem to Go

You say that it's over,
Your lips tell me so,
But each time that I try to leave
I just can't seem to go.

You say that it's over,
Our love's lost its glow,
But each time that I try to leave
I just can't seem to go.

You know that I love you,
Where did I go astray?
I remember our marriage vows,
It seems like yesterday.

How much do I love you?
Doesn't it show?
For each time that I try to leave,
I just can't seem to go.

Loneliness and sorrow became my garments.

Even Now

I've tried so hard to forget her,
I sometimes even wished that I had never met her,
But I know all too well that wish is a lie,
For the memory of her constantly passes me by.

I've tried to erase her from my mind,
But each time I try, I only find
That my imagination has caught me unaware
And I think I hear her footsteps on the stair.

When a love grows icy cold
And you feet its chilly blast,
What do you tell a broken heart
That wanted it to last?

Oh, I've tried to give my heart a gentle shove
By saying, surely you'll find another love,
But even now my heart remembers
And I, the fool, I fan the embers.

I'll Win Her Back

I'll win her back,
Just you wait and see.
I'll win her back,
My heart and me.

And I did.

Shortly after that she was diagnosed with multiple sclerosis.

These Few Precious Years

Her candle will be snuffed out long before it should,
And if I could give her some of my years I would,
But that is not part of His design,
And He shall take this love of mine.

The strength of her love is something I can't understand:
It belies the press of her frail hand.
But while she's still here, I am aware
That she has given me a love that's beyond compare.

And when He comes to take her away,
And she is placed beneath the clay,
I shall stand tall after I have wiped away all of my tears,
For I will have had her love for these few precious years.

Then came the forgotten war. This poem is dedicated to those Korean veterans.

The Objective

Our seemingly endless crosses row on row
Are highlighted by the full moon's glow.
Silent soldiers although our guns are still,
We want you to capture just one more hill.
Only then will we rest in peace
For at last we'll know that all wars shall cease.
Our crosses point out the objective for all to see:
We want the world to capture the hill of Calvary.

The civil rights movement.

Mine Eyes Have Seen the Glory

You brought me over from the Dark Continent in chains,
And at the end of the Civil War you said that I was free,
But you continued to shackle me.

Hate and prejudice became the new links of my chain:
You did not really set me free,
Instead you robbed me of my integrity.

My freedom was resolved,
A certain place to live, a certain place to toil,
When all I really owned was my final six feet of soil.

The South has been given time to heal the wounds of defeat.
That time has long passed and so little has been done for me,
I thought I won the victory!

"Mine eyes have seen the glory of the coming of the Lord..."
The next time you pause to pray,
What if a black angel were listening to what you had to say?

Silence?

Jesus said, "Love ye one another as I have loved you,"
And we cannot deny it, this fact is still true;
He didn't care what was the color of a man's skin.
He was so much wiser, He merely looked within.

To those of you who believe this truth
And you have mistakenly remained still,
Are you afraid that part of the journey will be uphill?

If you've been silent,
Now is the time to lift your voice.
God isn't offering you another choice.

Just listen to these words that Jesus is saying,
And then survey your loss:
"If you do not speak now, you would have remained silent
While I was being crucified on the cross."

Silence?

The Cuban crisis.

Hotline

When Kennedy and Khrushchev
Held the fate of the world in their hands,
I fell down on my knees
And I diligently prayed to God.
I didn't like humanity's odds.

As a result of that I wrote this, and I pray that it never happens:

After

After the last bomb has fallen in World War III,
I'll tell you this: for what it's worth,
The meek shall inherit the earth.

On Christmas Eve in 1965 a state highway patrolman came to our door and told me that my pa had been killed in a car accident. The short newspaper account could have added this.

He's Gone

He told me that everyone has a time and place
When they must meet death face to face.
A face that looked a lot like me
Has now become a memory.

My prayer is that the Lord's arms will enfold him,
Welcome him home, tenderly hold him,
For I know when death drew near
That he mocked the face of fear.

But oh, how I'll miss that grin
He always flashed when I walked in.
He always loved me, he seldom scolded,
And he took life as it unfolded.

And if there is one thing of which I am certain:
When death violently rang down its final curtain,
Perhaps he had time to cry out in pain,
But I know one thing: he didn't complain.

Our beloved dad, William "Lefty" Becker.

And then, just six months and fifteen days later.

She's Gone

She was slight of frame,
She weighed less than ninety pounds,
But she had a spirit
That surely knew no bounds.

As I stood by her bedside
And watched her grimace with pain,
At the time I didn't know
That her fight would be in vain.

For two long hours she battled death,
Fought it with all her might,
But the spark slowly dwindled
And at last out went the light.

We loved her so
And oh we wanted her to stay,
But we didn't ask Him why
When He took her away.

Now it's almost over,
But there is still this left to say:
For after the slow-moving procession
Had completed going its designated way,

As she approached her gravesite
I knew that my pa was no longer alone.
It was just as though he was saying,
"Welcome, welcome home."

Bertine "Berdie" Becker, we love you.

After her death I found four scraps of paper that she had used to figure her monthly budget on and they revealed that she had less than thirty dollars to live on. This poem is dedicated to her and to every widow who has ever gone to bed lonely and hungry.

Mrs. Becker, How Are You?

When you get old
And life has almost run its course,
And if the one you've loved is gone,
You too will sing a lonely song.

You get to know what loneliness is
Sitting alone in your room
Watching the shadows lengthen
As they mingle with the qloom.

Your friends will seldom call you,
For they've either moved or passed away,
And you've been wondering if you should use Colorback
To touch up the gray.

You budget and you plan,
For one hundred and six dollars a month
Doesn't go far:
There's never anything left for the cookie jar.

You talk to the dog
Or you pace the floor,
Waiting for that rare occasion
When there is a knock on the door.

You eat and sleep and cling to the past
Trying to recall every moment of happiness.
For now there are so few
Only the landlord seems glad to see you.

Oh, it's good to be wanted once a month,
Once a month when the rent is due.
He is even kind enough to ask,
"Mrs. Becker, how are you?"

Very few called her by her given name, and a few called her Bertina, but everyone else called her "Berdie."

Bertine "Berdie" Becker in Retrospect

My dad remarried when I was in Wendell Phillips Junior High School
And he chose a winner, he wasn't a fool.
We never called her "Mother," and that's a real shame,
Instead we always called her by her nickname.
She had many talents that she didn't use to the fullest degree,
This very thin and wonderful woman we called Berdie.

I can still see her buying a birthday card for my dad.
She probably spent every penny she had;
She looked at so many cards until she found just the right one,
I'd say that at least twenty minutes passed by before she was done.

She could cook, she could knit, she could darn and she could crochet,
But she used her greatest talent when she sat down at the piano to play:
She knew a multitude of songs, but no matter what she played,
When an audience gathered, they listened and they stayed.

When she arrived in Heaven I believe this scene took place soon:
The one where the good Lord turned to her and said "Berdie, play us a tune."
I know that when I see her I'll just say two words,
There won't be a need for any other, and those two words are, "Hello, Mother."

Martin Luther King, Jr.

He was an apostle of nonviolence
This gentle man of God,
And now he will no longer feel
The nightstick's hateful prod.

He was only on this earth
For thirty years and nine,
But he will be remembered
Throughout the eons of time.

He had a dream that one day
All of his people would be free,
For he knew this was the only way
That God intended it to be.

Let it be known that his death is also our shame,
For we, too, are in part to blame:
For after all is said and done,
Our apathy helped hold the assassin's gun.

We should no longer refuse
To put our feet in the black man's shoes,
For what a far better land this will be
When his dream becomes a reality.

He tried to make us realize
By opening up our callused eyes,
For he knew that it's still undeniably so
That we are our brother's keeper here below.

Yes ... and now above the shouts of white racism
God's unfailing voice is heard
As He issues this command with these fervent words,
"Sound the trumpets! Let the bells ring!
We are welcoming home Martin Luther King."

The Vietnam War (I was against the war but surely not against the veteran).

On This Day

On this day some men will die in Vietnam
And several abortions will take place.
Hurrah for the human race!

On this day lip-service for the black man will be said,
Just adding to the disgrace.
Hurrah for the human race!

On this day some of our youth
Will take another brash step away from God
By denying that He can see,
And thus compounding their own stupidity.

On this day we believe that we are much too wise
To abide by His irreplaceable rules,
And each nation continues to sail on man-made seas
That seem to have been charted by nothing but fools.

The Peace Marchers

They marched down the street
But there weren't any cheers.
The peace marchers carrying their signs
Were only greeted by jeers.

Yellow-bellied bastards and other words more choice,
Freedom was yelling with a lusty voice.
Throw a raw egg and run,
Hooray for freedom, this is fun.

Come on now, we'll break their damn desire,
Surely this small parade must be communistically inspired.
No more need be said,
Throw your eggs, aim for the head!

Yell at these peace marchers,
That is what they deserve.
All together now in unison,
You who line the curb.

If Jesus were to visit us
I know He would take a stand.
Do you think He would be jeering from the curb,
Or carrying a banner of peace in His hand?

My Lai

If I had been at My Lai
And I repeatedly fired my gun
Into the cowering crowd of the very old and young,
What ballad for me would be sung?
And if I were brought to trial,
How loud would the cheers be
If I were acquitted unanimously?

I could say that I'm not guilty
Ten thousand times a day
As if to deceive me.
The only trouble is that I would never really believe me,
My verdict would have been heaven-sent,
My indelible crime would be my punishment.

Part II

A Love Affair

I Fell in Love with April

I fell in love with April,
I wooed her thirty days.
I fell in love with April
In spite of her fickle ways.

I still recall her laughter
Dancing on the air.
And smell the scent of lilacs
Coming from her hair.

I fell in love with April,
She made my whole world glow.
I melted down her resistance
Just like the winter snow.

I fell in love with April,
But now that she's gone away,
I guess I'll have to fall
In love with May.

The courtship of Linda Carol Odegaard.

I Have Known

I have known more sorrow
Than you will ever know,
And that is why I'm asking you
To bid me stay or go.

And when I give you something to read,
Pause before you start,
Don't merely read it with your eyes,
Read it with your heart.

What Am I Going To Do With You?

What am I going to do with you?
For my very being you have entwined,
And now you have captured this heart of mine.

What am I going to do with you?
For when you turn to walk away,
My heart cries out,
"Please stay! Please stay!"

What am I going to do with you?
For every time I look into your eyes,
I'm afraid that I'll wake the room,
Just by the way my heart sighs.

What am I going to do with you?
For every moment, how I yearn,
And now I have reached the point of no return.

The Plan

Like a spider spinning an intricate web,
I too have a plan ahead
For whether you're near me
Or we're far apart,
I long to ensnare you
In the web of my heart.

The Hourglass

My love for you is like an hourglass.
For knowing all the while
That if the glass is emptying,
You turn it over when you smile.

Puppets

The first time I met you
I knew from the start
That my words would become puppets
Moved by the strings of my heart.

If You Were Mine

If you were mine,
Each night before sleep finally closed your eyes
You would become aware and realize
That your heart had been given a constant shove
And that you were truly loved.

And I handed this to her.

The Note

If you were to take a drink
From the well of my heart,
Each time that you returned,
You would pause with a start!
For you would have to confess
That now there was more
When logically, there should be less.

Ah, but that is the way
My heart had it planned,
And with this note
I've placed the dipper in your hand.

How Can I Tell You?

Some people say that I have the gift of gab,
That I'm a master at using words,
But I'd be the first to readily admit
Their hasty assumption is absurd.

How can I tell you
All you mean to me?
How can I tell you?
How can I make you see?

How can I tell you?
What can my lips say
To express my love for you
In a different way?

In this heart of mine
I hear words to say,
But when you appear
All of them fade away.

I long to tell you
But each time that I start,
I get all tied up
In the web of your heart.

Perhaps this will make you lean, until you fall.

When

When are you going to realize,
That I look at you through different eyes?
Like waves that pound on a distant shore,
My heart demands that I give you more.

When are you going to become aware,
That I am offering you a love that is rare?
And just like a duelist, I demand satisfaction.
Let me make you the center of my heart's attraction.

Come With Me

Come with me if your heart has been lonely,
And if you've been waiting to give love a try;
Come with me, come with me, my darling,
Oh, incidentally so have 1.

Come to me if your lips have been longing
To be pressed and to know the reason why;
Come to me, come to me, my darling,
For, needless to say, so have 1.

The heart is a lonely hunter
And time is its hourglass,
And while the grains have shifted so slowly,
Now you'll find that they'll fall all too fast.

So run to me if your heart has been waiting
For true love to knock on its door;
Run to me, run to me, my darling
And I'll love you forevermore.

A Falling Star

My world with its gloom,
Its anxiety and its strife,
Faded like a falling star,
Trailing into the night.
My world like that star,
Became suddenly bright.

And to think that this star
That fell upon my heart
Might have missed me,
Except for the endearing fact
That you had just kissed me.

And my thoughts continued to chase you down the hallways of my heart.

There Will Be Other Moments

There will be other moments,
Moments just like this.
There will be other moments
When our lips meet in a kiss.

There will be other moments
That we can hold dear,
And soon the sound of wedding bells
You and I will hear.

I'll give you a love that you can cherish
Until your dying day.
There will be other moments,
Though this moment slips away.

Time will prove I love you,
More than all I'll ever possess,
For you alone will be my own,
My life, my happiness.

When we first met, did she think this of me?

In His Arms

As a girl I played with dolls
In a land where dreams came true.
I didn't have a worry or a care,
For life was vibrant and new.

But soon the years passed by
And I no longer was that little girl.
True, I still had dreams, but of the man
Who would set my heart in a whirl.

I waited patiently
With my two feet on the ground,
But soon my head was in the clouds,
For this is what I found.

In his arms I discovered
All a love could ever be.
In his arms I uncovered
What true love alone can see.

In his arms I uncovered
Feelings I had never known.
In his arms I discovered
I didn't want to be alone.

And after his lips met mine
And while I breathed a sigh,
He whispered, "I love you,"
And there was no one happier than 1.

In his arms I uncovered
All of the dreams that had flown,
In his arms I discovered
A love that was mine alone.

The answer to my question has to be no.

The Journey

Each one of us is taking a trip
That will be filled with laughter and strife
As we journey down the road
That we choose to call life.

My heart has always been a rover,
Searching for a love that would be
As wide as the uncharted sky
And as deep as the sea.

I eagerly set forth
But I was fooled by some sighs,
And I had to wipe away some tears
From my reddened eyes.

Then when I least expected it,
I wasn't on the rebound,
He came into my life
And this is what I found.

Now the journey is over,
Nevermore will I roam,
For when his arms beckoned to me,
I knew that my heart had found its home.

This is a shade closer.

The First Time

Some people believe in love at first sight
But I have to disagree,
And this is the reason why
First impressions are not for me.

The first time I met him
He didn't impress me too much,
But soon I discovered
That I longed for his touch.

From the first time we dated
He was so thoughtful and kind
That soon I realized
He always had me in mind.

He didn't have to say much
To change my initial point of view,
And in a very short while
I could say that I knew.

For the first time he kissed me
I saw the world from above,
And for the last time
The very last time, I fell in love.

We're out of the shade now, this became a reality.

And how was it for me?

When I Was Young

When I was young
I had dreams that burned like fire,
Dreams that were fanned by my youthful desire
When I was young.

When I was young
I believed I could do any task.
All someone had to do was just ask,
When I was young.

When I was young
I dreamt of many things:
I ran the gauntlet from cabbages to kings.
But the older I became,
The more my dreams began to mellow
Just like an ordinary fellow.

I was so all alone until I met you,
And then I discovered that my dreams began anew,
And when you gave your heart to me
For all the world to see,
My dreams were like beads that had to be strung.
I never had a dream like this before
When I was young.

This surely hits the mark.

What Did She Ever See in Me?

They say that love is blind,
And I agree.
As a matter of fact, for evidence
I offer me.

What did she ever see in me
To even take a second glance?
And when she first saw my funny face,
Why did she decide to take a chance?

What did she ever see in me
That no one else had seen before?
And when she looked into my eyes,
Did I convey that much and more?

And when these clumsy hands of mine
Took and held her in my arms,
What could I have possibly said
To extol all of her charms?

What did she ever see in me?
I'll ask for the rest of my life.
For she not only relented, she consented,
And became my loving wife.

Jill

Linda, I must confess,
That a new woman has come into my life,
And I thought that there would never be another.
But I'm asking you to forgive me
Because she looks an awful lot like her mother.

I Never Thought

I never thought that I'd have a child to hold,
But I do now, and I'm fifty years old.
And she has become more than just a part of me,
For she has captured the very heart of me.

Michael

We named him Michael.

On the day of departure,
Linda and he took the mandatory wheel chair ride
From the hospital exit to our open car door;
And as they approached the car radio was playing
"Michael Row the Boat Ashore."

We knew, we didn't have to guess,
Surely we had been twice blessed.

Part III

Thorns and Roses

Where I used to work the brass wanted me to be less than I am. They willfully gave me more prolonged mental anguish than I knew as a combat infantryman.

They knew I was hurting, but they continued to pour salt in my wounds. When I asked for justice they did just as they pleased When I asked for bread they gave me a stone. Their cold callousness made me feel like I was a distant cousin of Job and it resulted in this.

Forsaken

Sometimes when your so-called friends forsake you,
It can do more than just hurt,
It can break you.

When You've Got the Blues

Life has its ups and downs,
Its change of mood and shade;
And sometimes blue and only blue
Is the color being displayed.

When the blues have got you down
And you're feeling awfully low
Because you've just hit the bottom,
And that's as far as you can go.

You can try to drown your sorrow,
And that may help for a day,
But you'll still have the blues
Long after your hangover has gone away.

And as for that silver lining
That's still hiding behind a cloud,
It finds others too are waiting
But you believe you head the crowd.

For when you're feeling down and out
And you hate being in your shoes,
That silver lining can be so elusive
'Specially when you've got the blues.

When I Die

When I die
And leave this planet,
I don't want my name or dates
Chiseled on my piece of granite.

I hope that my death is still years away–
Then again, it could be today or tomorrow–
But no matter when, I want my inscription to be thus:

A MAN
OF
SORROW

I Truly Am

I do not believe that God is dead
No matter what they say,
For I felt His presence when my parents
Were placed beneath the clay.

Life's pathways with their intricate design
Have made me taste the bittersweet, often the unkind,
But lest you think that I am unique,
Not one iota of your sympathy do I seek:
For as you pass through these fleeting years
You too will have filled your cup with tears.

Sometimes I have to wryly smile
When I think of man's insidious guile,
And yet I laugh and I sing as if out of necessity
Until that final bell tolls for me.
I do not know if I will be granted tomorrow,
But this I know, I truly am a man of sorrow.

Sometimes

I do care what befalls me,
But no matter what the demand
I shall not let go of His hand.

I shall not question His design,
Although there are many things that I don't understand,
I shall not let go of His hand.

But lately I must admit
That when I take all that has happened
And weigh it on life's scales,
Sometimes I feel like I have been crucified
Without any nails.

The Aftermath

It would have to take someone who had really been hurt to write those anguished poems. If I had to do it all over again I wouldn't have written a couple of them. I couldn't omit them, though.

I continued to hurt after I retired from there, but the good Lord and my precious family and a new workplace saw me through the slow healing process.

Unfortunately, because of their demeaning actions at work, this was partly true.

Your Knock

I'm sure that everyone knows
At least one of these,
The fool who cannot see
The forest for the trees.

I was a fool, my love,
For I had you,
And yet like a restless wave at sea
I didn't know what to do.

I kept on fumbling and stumbling around,
Searching and seeking, not knowing that I had found
That you were all that I need, and now I concede,
As the years pass me by,
My heart can only say, "What a fool was 1!"

I kept on searching and seeking,
Not knowing just exactly what for,
And all the while
You were knocking on my heart's door.

But now, my love,
I want the world to see
What I will do with the time
That's still allotted to me.

I shall give you all of my love,
And so much more,
Knowing that this fool
Should have answered your knock long before.

This I Know

When the mirror of your dreams has been shattered
And life's pendulum has swung all the way
From the white to the black,
This I know:
Put your trust in Him,
And the pendulum will
                    swing
          back.

Broken Pieces

He took all of the broken pieces of my life
And He lovingly made them whole,
So the world could see
The triumph of a soul.

Just like the incoming tide, this thought persisted until I realized...

I'm Not My Whole Self

A half does not become a whole
Until it's loved with all a heart and soul.

I talk to people,
But I know all the while
I'm not my whole self
Until I see you smile.

I look at faces,
But it's so plain to see,
I'm not my whole self
Until you are with me.

For when I'm with you,
My life is complete:
Just hear the thunder
Of my every heartbeat.

It may be crowded,
But I'm so all alone.
I'm not my whole self
Until your arms welcome me home.

David

We didn't know what to call him at first,
But we finally decided that David would be his name,
And believe me, our world has never been the same.
We knew that we had been blessed from above
For now we had three precious children to love.

Outside of Our House

Outside of our house
There's an old lilac tree
That has seen far better times,
Just between you and me.

Outside of our house
There's a garden with weeds, so to speak,
My mommy insists that vegetables
Love to play hide-and-go-seek.

Outside of our house
There's a broken window that my dad's going to mend.
Just as soon as he's through
Helping some old friend.

Our house is the smallest one on the block,
But my brothers and I, we don't care what you say:
We wouldn't trade it for a mansion.
We want it that way.

For inside of our house
There are two added ingredients
We place far above,
Our house is filled with laughter and love.

The Years That Have Passed Us By

The years that have passed us by
Have found that our love has grown:
Not every dream has come true,
But not one of them has flown.

The years that have passed us by
Have shown us that love should never he
Like a fire that's left unattended
It must be rekindled constantly.

All too many a love
That was once a burning fire
Loses its glow and dies,
As the years slowly transpire.

I love you so much, my darling,
And there's so much more to be said.
And I'll continue to do so
In the years that lie ahead.

This poem is dedicated to Linda for every one of our anniversaries.

As You Were

When our love was new
I wondered if it would prevail;
Then I stopped and took another look,
When I was farther down life's trail.

As you were, as you were,
I fell in love with you
For you were, for you were,
A dream come true.

I recall, I recall
One wonderful day,
When you promised to love,
Honor and obey.

Years have passed, years have passed,
And with the passing of time,
I'm aware, I'm aware,
Now that I find

As you are, as you are,
I can only say:
I love you more,
I love you more today.

My Sister

My sister means the world to me,
And I know that if you could look inside, you would see
A heart that really cares,
But one who has also had to climb some lonely stairs.

The man who killed our dad
Because he tried to drive after drinking far too many beers,
I want him to know, that if they could have been accumulated
He could have taken a bath in her tears.

My sister's Biblical roots run deep,
And although at times the grade has been steep,
With His guidance she has been able to withstand,
Even when cancer took her by the hand.

She and her husband Joe
Always bring the sunshine with them wherever they go,
And when the grandchildren come to their house to play,
You can be sure that their little hearts have come to stay.

We used to fight when we were small.
We would chase each other up and down the hall;
She would pull hair, kick and scratch.
I don't recall ever winning a match.

But as the years passed by we didn't have to let it be known,
That our love for each other had constantly grown,
For I know that if you were to take a look,
You would find that we're as close as two opposite pages in a book.

Let There Be Hope in Your Heart

Let there be hope in your heart
With each new dawning day.
Whatever your dreams command,
Let your heart obey.

Let there be hope in your heart,
No matter what's your fate.
You can untangle the web:
It's never too late.

The dreams that have fled,
They can still come true.
They're at your beck and call,
It all depends on you.

For if there is hope in your heart
Then no matter, come what may,
The world will have been a better place
Just because of you today.

Part IV

Laughter and Tears

Office Parties

If this place ever catches on fire,
We're going to be in one heck of a fix
Because we've been using
The extinguishers for a mix

Dear Abby

I'm writing a letter to Abby,
And I know just what I'll say:
"I followed your instruction precisely,
How come my mother-in-law still plans to stay?"

(Not really, she's a wonderful person.)

Let Us Come to Our Census

I'm against abortion
And I'll tell you the reason why:
If my parents had had the choice,
I might not have been an I.

I Boo

I boo
The A.C.L.U.

Puppy Love

Let's all be as loving
As a newborn pup:
Instead of giving them the finger,
Let's give'em the thumbs up.

Longevity

My doctor told me that pain won't kill you,
And although I reluctantly agree,
I don't think that it's going to add to my longevity.

The Cowboy

When Western wear became popular,
My wife put her hand to her brow.
For when I tried on a cowboy hat
She exclaimed, “You look more like the cow!”

The Eager Beaver

If I were a beaver
And you were a tree,
I'd whittle at you, baby,
Until you fell for me.

Let the chips fall where they may,
I love you more than I can say.

Your Heart's Door

I'm sure that I woke up the whole neighborhood,
The way the noise resounded,
For when I approached your heart's door,
I didn't knock, I pounded!

The Rest of Your Life

I thought that you loved me
All of these years,
But what you just told me
Has me in tears.

I never thought that
You'd cheat or lie,
But now you confess
That you've been seeing him on the sly.

You're having an affair with another,
And still you want me to stay.
All you need is more time,
You don't want me to go away.

You have to get him out of your system
And then you'll be my loving wife,
You don't know how long it's going to take you,
But I do–you've got the rest of your life.

This poem was written for the 50th reunion of the 102nd Infantry Division.

Camp Maxie 1942

I just have to tell you about my thirteen weeks of basic training,
For eleven of them it seemed like it was constantly raining.

Oh, the Captain, Captain, Captain said it to me,
I was the best damned soldier in the infanantry,
I must admit that I was as surprised as I could be,
When I spent the first three weeks of my Basic on K.P.

Oh, the Captain, Captain, Captain said it to me,
I was the best damned soldier in the infanantry,
He told me that I was the finest that he'd ever seen,
The finest spent the next three weeks cleaning up the latrine.

Oh, the Captain, Captain, Captain said it to me,
I was the best damned soldier in the infanantry,
When it comes to soldiering, I was a beauty,
Guess who spent the next three weeks walking guard duty?

Oh, the Captain, Captain, Captain said it to me,
I was the best damned soldier in the infanantry.
He told me that I was a cut above the rest, but now I needed a change
I spent the next three weeks on bivouac and the last one on the rifle range.

When I limped back to the barracks,
I didn't know what was going to be the Captain's next order,
But I knew that our camp was located near the Mexican border
And that's when I decided to give the Captain a thrill,
And the best damned soldier went over the hill.

With What's-Her-Name

We had our first quarrel
Just before the senior hop.
Foolishly we let it get out of hand
And we didn't know when to stop.

The lights are turned down low
And you see me with my new flame.
You think I wish I were holding you,
But I'm dancing with What's-her-name.

The lights are turned down low
And you believe it's still the same.
You think I wish it were you instead,
But I'm dancing with What's-her-name.

You didn't think I'd forget you,
I can see it in your eyes.
You didn't think I'd forget you,
Now I hope you realize.

The music has stopped playing
And I'm so awfully glad I came
Just so I could show that I've forgotten you,
I'm going to leave with What's-her-name.

You Could Be a Movie Queen

You could be a movie queen,
Be the star of stage and screen,
I know you could
Be the toast of Hollywood.

And while I'm pretending,
Suppose I complete the plan:
I can picture you in a love scene
With me as your leading man.

A scene with hundreds of kisses
That began at break of day,
And when that scene is over
I know just what I'll say:

"Hey, Mr. Director! Mr. Director!
For my sake
Let's have another,
Let's have another retake."

Sometimes circumstance finds a person looking at their world through hurting eyes.

Maybe one of the three following poems for men or one of the three following poems for women can become like shoes for you to walk in, but after you do, read "To Be Loved." This is my wish for you.

For the men:

Now You Pass Me By

There was a time, my darling,
When you tried to catch my eye.
You wanted me for your own,
But now you pass me by.

There was a time, my darling,
When my kiss could make you sigh.
You said it was forever,
But now you pass me by.

Time sure changes everything,
All the things that used to be:
For now you're with another,
How I wish that it were me.

If I should say "I don't love you"
I'd be telling you a lie.
My lonely arms still want you,
But now you pass me by.

Whose Arms Did You Fall Out Of Now?

At one time you were my darling,
But you chose to break every vow,
And now you come running back to me–
Whose arms did you fall out of now?

Your latest affair is over,
I heard it ended with a row,
And now you come running back to me–
Whose arms did you fall out of now?

They say that time heals everything
And this is almost true,
But then you show up and fill my cup
With memories of you.

Each time I hope that you'll remain,
Perhaps I'll find a way somehow,
I long for the day I won't have to say,
"Whose arms did you fall out of now?"

She Came Running Back to Me

She came running back to me
But I know that she won't stay:
My eager arms will only hold her
Until someone new comes her way.

She knows how much I've missed her,
And she knows how much I care,
But all too soon, like autumn trees,
My arms will be empty and bare.

For a while I'll thrill to her kiss
And I will hear her sigh,
But unfortunately, all too soon
I will hear her say goodbye.

I know that I'm just a fool in love,
And that my heart will never learn,
Until the day that she decides
Never to return.

For the ladies:

This Isn't the Way

This isn't the way
That I had it planned:
I didn't intend
To lose my man.

I must admit
That I don't know why,
For no one can love him
Deeper than I.

I wanted our love to grow
Through the years,
But today it all ended
With me in tears.

I can still hear those unwanted words,
"I don't love you anymore,"
Followed by his final
Closing of the door.

Somewhere Between

Somewhere between "I do"
And "I'm sorry"
There has to be
A sad love story.

Somewhere between "always"
And "it's over,"
There must have been a time
When his heart wasn't a rover.

Somewhere between "I do"
And "it's ended"
There's still a broken heart
That hasn't mended.

For my whole world crumbled to bits
When he said, "Let's call it quits."
My support group seems to understand
It's hard to go through no man's land.

Now I know the past doesn't end
With the closing of a door:
Instead it becomes your shadow
While you pace the floor.

Where Does Love Go?

Where does love go when it dies,
And it's no longer seen in each other's eyes?

Where does love go when it turns to hate,
And it slams shut reconciliation's gate?

Where does love go when there are tears,
And you cry so loud but nobody hears?

Where does love go when "until death do us part,"
No longer is the main concern of the heart?

Where does love go when your whole world revolves around him oh so much
And now he mistakenly thinks that he needs a much younger touch?

Where does love go when it decides to cheat,
And it marches to an adulterous beat?

Where does love go when you tearfully box up the toys,
And you know it's the children that divorce destroys?

Where does love go when you know you've lived a lie,
And you realize that it didn't have to end–you let it die?

Where does love go when you still cherish the prize?
It goes to the look that is seen in each other's eyes.

In the following poem the men will have to read: "She'll be by your side."

To Be Loved

Dreams are a dime a dozen,
And with this thought in mind,
After life has sorted all of yours out
May this be what you find...

To be loved and to love
Is the greatest thing,
To know that this isn't
Just another fling.

To be loved and to love,
Knowing that he'll be by your side
Just as long as there are stars
That refuse to hide.

Surmounting each obstacle,
Overcoming every care,
Letting your dreams intermingle,
For now they are yours to share.

To be loved and to love
Until you've become completely aware
That your love has slipped
Out of the ordinary and into the rare,
To be loved, to be loved, to be loved.

Part V

Nearing the Journey's End

Daybreak

The day is starting to awaken,
Soon the dawn will be breaking,
The eastern sky is tinged with red,
Soon the night will be dead.
The birds are whistling a serenade,
Just listen to how fully it's being played
And as the sun peeks over the ridge of a hill,
Each noise slowly subsides until all is still,
There is a reverent pause

While the world silently applauds.

A Winter Morning Walk

He covered all of the trees with crystals of ice today,
And they sparkled like diamonds all along the way.
But then the sun came out with a wide grin,
And slowly gathered all of them in.

The Crucifixion

Jesus knelt down and prayed in Gethsemane,
Saying, "Father, if it be possible, let this cup pass from me."
James and John and Peter were fast asleep,
His darkest hour was His alone to keep.
He knew that the cup would not pass,
But He wasn't dismayed.
The hour had come for Him to be betrayed:
Judas came, a kiss,
Nothing more, simply this.

At His trial He was all alone,
Alone as He could be.
He was forced to relive His Gethsemane.
And after the angry mob had its fill
He took that painful walk to Golgotha hill.

At the sixth hour darkness covered the land,
It was an ominous thing,
And dying on the cross
Was Jesus Christ the King!

Easter Vacation

We're bound for Florida ground,
We're headed for the beach,
For a grand and glorious vacation
That will soon be within our reach.

We'll have everything that we hold dear,
The booze, the broads and the ice cold beer;
And we'll pull down many a halter top
So that we can laugh when we see them flop.

Georgie Porgie tonight we're going to have
Another drunken orgy
And no one is going to make us cease,
Not even the nightly clashes with the police.

Empty beer cans clutter the beach,
And other litter by the ton
That was deliberately left there
By the so-called educated ones.

Empty sand, the beaches are bare,
The bikini-clad, the good and bad
Have finally deserted you;
Alas, your glorious vacation is through.

Yes, it was a lovely Easter vacation,
But after all is said and done,
Too few of you failed to heed its message,
You never saw the risen Son.

The Figurehead

All too often we do not thirst
For the One whom we should put first.
We toast the superfluous glitter of the world instead,
And we mistakenly make Him just a figurehead.

No Longer

I thought I would never say this,
And to make matters worse,
It won't even cause a sensation:
We no longer are a Christian nation.

The following poem will verify that fact.

If You Could Go Back

If you could go back to that point in time
When you felt the warmth of your mother's womb,
And if you still had several months to stay
Within that solitary room
And if she were seriously thinking about having an abortion,
And you could speak, this would be your impassioned plea,
"Mother, dear mother, please don't abort me."

We have silenced thirty-eight million little voices and to compound that fact of shame, we are still counting.

I don't know exactly where this poem belongs chronologically, but it does belong.

I Used To Be a Wayward One

I used to be a wayward one,
But then one day,
Just as sure as you please,
He put me on His anvil of grace,
And with His hammer of love He beat me
Until I found myself down on my knees.

When I got up I wasn't the same man
That I was before:
My soul had fought a treacherous foe
And it had won the war.
Some old habits ended immediately,
And yet I knew others would be hard to break,
But I knew that I could do it,
No matter how long it would take.
For deep down within,
I knew for the very first time
That I would try to do His will
And not mine.

The Closet

Every now and then I enter one of the closets of mind,
And I take down some of the sins that I've placed
On an all too familiar shelf,
And I painfully rerun them through my mind,
Because I still haven't forgiven myself.

The Vietnam Memorial

The way we treated the Vietnam veteran is a national disgrace. On November 13, 1982, the long-overdue Vietnam Veterans Memorial was dedicated and it contained the names of over 58, 000 of our dead. I believe that we ruined more Vietnam veterans' lives than those whose names appear on the black granite walls because of our cold and callous indifference. This poem is dedicated to the Vietnam veterans.

The Veterans Hospital Psycho Ward B

Somewhere you lost a page in time
And reality has flown.
The dreams that once you shared
Have now become yours alone.
Somewhere in the prison house of your mind
The patterns of thought have become confused,
And although people are trying to help you,
That help is often refused.
They want you to understand
But you don't even understand yourself.
They are trying to figure out your processes of thought,
But you've misplaced them on some dusty forgotten shelf.

Some are old who enter here,
And they live in the past;
Reality comes every now and then,
But it never seems to last.
Their hair is gray,
Their step is slow,
As up and down, up and down
The corridors they go.

Time will not heal many,
For them, time is a curse.
Instead of getting better,
Most of them will get worse.
Deep in and out of thought
Their footsteps echo down the hall,
And thus they will continue to walk
Until they hear the Master's call.

Some are young who enter there,
But not if you look inside.
The scars of war have aged them,
And from reality they want to hide.
Once reality was theirs,
But with every twisted body that came into view,
For some it was too much
And their minds became twisted, too.
Some of these muddled minds
Will never again know inward peace.
For them the cannons will always roar,
And the war will never cease.
War is hell's mistress,
And they fight it daily in their mind.
Life is a precious thing,
But for some, death is kind.

If all of us could walk through each ward,
Then perhaps at last our eyes would really see,
And the quicksilver search for peace
Would no longer be a travesty.
But if this doesn't do the trick,
If your callous conscience isn't pricked,
Then may your every dream
End like theirs–with an anguished scream!
Then at last you would become aware
And every sword would be beaten into a plowshare.

May You Always Be a Dreamer

In this world of the speeded-up pace,
Where we act just as though we're running a race,
Hurrying from or scurrying to,
Stop! A moment...
And I'll bequeath this legacy to you.

May you always be a dreamer,
Reaching for a distant star.
May you never be content
With things just the way they are.

May you always be a dreamer,
Longing for the promise of spring.
May it always be your desire
To find a love song you can sing.

May your dreams never mellow,
Or be placed in the shade,
Always wear them proudly,
Like a banner being displayed.

May you always be a dreamer,
Even when your hair has turned gray.
May you still be like a spider,
And spin a new dream every day.

The Last Veteran

We interrupt this program to bring you this special reporl. With the death of Roy Jackson of Huntsville, Alabama, Herman Mueller has become the last living World War One veteran. He is being questioned by the press. We join the program in progress.

Just a short while ago you didn't even know that I did exist,
And now you tell me how much I will be missed.
You've asked me which war slogan I liked the best,
Which one would I choose over all of the rest,
"A war to end all wars,"
Or "A war to make the world safe for democracy."
Believe me, I wouldn't choose either one,
For that would be hypocrisy.

We had ll6, 516 casualties.
Germany, Russia, France and Austria-Hungary's combined
casualties topped six million.
And when you add to the carnage at least twenty-one million
wounded, there is only one slogan that will do:
"Cannon fodder, pass in review!"

And now I have to tell you more about my precious wife. One Christmas season Linda gave me this:

> ***<u>The Wife's Christmas List</u>***
>
> *Black gloves*
>
> *Socks*
>
> *Coffee maker (if you can find one that isn't too expensive)*
>
> *But you don't have to get me anything, dear–*
> *you are enough.*

My List

I was going to make a long list
Of the things that I was thankful for,
But I only managed to write down just one.
For when I tried to thank Him for my Linda,
I discovered
That it couldn't
Be done.

If we hadn't attended a dance at our Employees Club this would have never been written.

Unless Linda

You think that you're a ladies' man,
That no woman could resist.
You want me to introduce her to you,
As a matter of fact, you insist.

When you meet her you'll smile
And she'll do the same.
I know you'll sense a thrill
When she speaks your name.

You can take her on the dance floor,
She'll give your heart a whirl.
You'll be glad you met her,
More than any other girl.

You can tell her your jokes,
For her laughter is like spring,
But don't be mistaken,
For it won't mean a thing.

You can look into her eyes
But you will never see
The look of love, unless
Linda is looking at me.

We Have Known Love

Most of my life is behind me,
While most of hers still lies ahead;
And all too soon the swift hand of time will pass,
And I shall be dead...

But we have known a love
All too few ever know.
In the spring and autumn of our lives,
Our steps haven't been slow.
For we've been building memories
Of every different kind,
So later she can run them through
The hourglass of her mind.

For we have found a love
All too few ever attain:
Imagine finding such a love,
A love that wasn't in vain.
Some of her youth has rubbed off on me,
And we two have loved to the Nth degree,
But you can't fool Father Time,
He will be coming after me.

So while there is still time
We will lift the cup,
Knowing that I won't be allowed
To drink all of mine up,
For that's the way life is,
And the way it will always be.
So I humbly thank the Lord
For giving such a love to me.

Even more so now.

A Cloudy Day

I don't care if it's cloudy,
For the sunshine of your smile
Always casts a shadow
Across my heart's sundial.

Then and Now

I was in the autumn of my years,
While hers were still in the spring,
At first we chatted idly and it didn't mean a thing.
There were younger suitors dating her, I knew;
But as time passed by, a spark between us grew,
And then one day when she spoke my name,
The spark ignited and it burst into a flame.
I courted her with all the fullness of my life,
Until at last, she became my loving wife.

Now the shadows have lengthened,
And because you can't turn back the hands of time,
All too soon that final bell for me will chime.
Therefore I want the press of my hand,
To let her know, to make her understand,
So that it won't have to be verbally said
That all too soon, I will have to go ahead.
Therefore my one wish is that there will be
Many other loves just as great as ours,
For we have reached out our hands,
And we have touched the stars.

The Stairway

If you were to take the time
To climb the stairway of my mind,
I know this is what you will find.

A lot of laughter and some tears,
And a little bit of knowledge
That I've gleaned through the years.
Ah, but this one thing,
All else above,
You are surely going to find love.

My Love for You

My love for you will never be
As constant as the tide,
For the word "steady" is the connotation
That's being implied,
And that, my love for you could never be,
Because each day it grows with more intensity.

Especially

Love is a necessary ingredient for life,
For without it we are dead
And it doesn't matter how many years still lie ahead.
For without love there can't be any compassion,
And we'll never understand that life should be lived to the fullest.
This should be our heart's command
And in order to do that, there are three indispensable traits
That we should adhere to like a hand in a glove,
And they are understanding and compassion but especially love.

April 13,1989

I'm sixty-six years old today
And I am amazed at how time flies,
Stolen like the Biblical thief,
And right before my very eyes.

My birthday finds that my emotions
Have become like melted butter.
I guess in part I'm wondering
If I'll be granted yet another.

And as for the ones I love,
I love them so much more,
I find myself pounding
On their hearts' door.

Let me in! It's getting late!
You won't have to strike a match.
To open your heart's door,
Just undo the latch.

Undo the latch
And let me stay,
Even after He
calls me
away.

The Days of December

When I am with you the length of my days
Are like those in December and not the month of June,
For I find that they always end much too soon.

There Isn't a Day

There isn't a day that I don't hurt,
Sometimes I feel like I'm having pain for dessert.
My knees, my back, my neck and my shoulder,
Are only unfriendly reminders that I've gotten older.
But I'm not going to let it get me down,
Because I have too much to be thankful for,
To ever wear a frown.

If they paid for pain I would be a very wealthy man.

Before I reach my journey's end, my heart insists that I say this.

Soon

Soon it will be time for me to go
And you will have to stay.
But before He calls me home
There are some things that I must say.
You have given me three precious children,
A daughter and two sons,
You have given me a love
That is second to none.
The meaningful hugs,
The lingering kiss,
The looks of love
That have added to the bliss.
The sound of laughter,
The happy tears,
A love that has grown
Throughout the years.
What a woman,
What a lover,
What a mother,
What a wife:
You have given new meaning
To the word "life."

Those of you who know me,
Can say that I've done some stupid things,
And that all too often I've played
The buffoon in my life,
But one thing you have to grant me,
I know how to choose a wife.

Maybe

Maybe because of my boundless love for her,
I won't feel the tug of death upon my sleeve,
And I'll be granted a few more precious years,
Before He decides that it's my time to leave.

Valentine's Day 1997

What Can I Tell You?

What can I tell you?
How can I possibly convey
All of the love
That I have for you today?
I'm completely at a loss,
For no matter what my choice
Of words might be,
They would be inadequate
Because I can see
That with each new dawning day
I love you all the more,
And I'm still searching
For the words to use
From the day before.

The first line of this poem is exactly the same as one of the lines that I wrote for my dad. I wanted it that way.

Shoes

And if there is one thing of which I am certain,
Before I am placed beneath the sod,
I know beyond the shadow of a doubt,
That there is a caring and loving God.

When man-inflicted pain became so intense,
That for a time my senses almost took leave,
But through all the doubt and the confusion,
He kept tugging on my sleeve.

Some of you might have wondered, "How can you believe?"
But that was because you only saw the strife
And not any of the times that He intervened
Throughout this wayward Pilgrim's life.

For He took this human vessel
And He tested it with flame
And when I emerged from the fire I was His,
And I've never been the same.

My faith became as tall and strong
As the legendary Lebanon cedars of old,
And He did that for this lost sheep
When He welcomed me back into the fold.

There have been several times in my life
When I looked into Death's beckoning face,
And each one that I recall
Only reminds me of His amazing grace.

I want you to believe what I say,
For if you don't, that would be your greatest loss.
You would have turned your back on the One
Who died for you on a blood-stained cross.

Yes, it's been quite a journey,
And if you could have walked it in my shoes,
Just like Paul and Silas,
You would have to spread the good news.

Let It Begin

If I were granted but one wish
I know what I would say:
"Let's have a grand and glorious revival,
And let it begin today!"

The Recipe

Two ingredients that are essential for livin'
Are to forgive and to be forgiven.

I Believe

I don't know how often it happened,
But every now and then
I believe that He guided my pen.

How Do You Measure Love?

How do you measure love?
Can you put it in a jar?
Does it look the same up close
As it does from afar?

How do you measure love?
Is it like a bird in flight
That suddenly appears
And then quickly fades from sight?

How do you measure love?
Can you press it in a book
And will it still be there
When you take another took?

How do you measure love?
There is just one place to start
And that is in the secret
Recesses of the heart.

What Am I Going to Do?

When you are young,
The sands of time shift slow.
But when you get old,
You wonder, where did they go?

What am I going to do
With the rest of my life?
For the sun will be setting soon
In the west of my life.

What am I going to do
With the dreams that have flown?
Will I continue to chase them,
Or leave them alone?

What am I going to do
Now that my step is slow?
Which way should I turn?
Which way should I go?

Then all of a sudden it hit me
Like the slap from a duelist's glove:
I'll fill all of the rest of my days
With love.

Epilogue

If the end result of this journey has made you look at the world through gentler and more caring eyes–wonderful. If it has made you take a continuous step toward Him I couldn't ask for more. I know I should have taken mine long before.

Peace and much love.